J Fic   COP   5
 Luderer, Lynn Marie.
The toad intruder.

Houghton, 1982
   46 p. : ill. ;

The
Toad Intruder

The
Toad Intruder

LYNN MARIE LUDERER

Illustrated by Diane de Groat

Houghton Mifflin Company
Boston 1982

Library of Congress Cataloging in Publication Data

Luderer, Lynn Marie.
The toad intruder.

Summary: Although Monica would like her toad Schultz
to need her as much as her dog and her hamster do, she
comes to believe he would be happier in the woods.
[1. Toads—Fiction.   2. Pets—Fiction] I. DeGroat,
Diane, ill.   II. Title.
PZ7.L9749To   [Fic]   81-13397
ISBN 0-395-32081-X   AACR2

Printed in the United States of America
P 10 9 8 7 6 5 4 3 2 1

For my mother

The
Toad Intruder

Monica Bottleby was nine years old and she liked animals. In fact, Monica liked animals a lot better than she liked people. She didn't play with the girls on the block, and she didn't play with the boys either. The only people she played with were Hamlet and Howard. Hamlet was a hamster, and Howard was a dog.

The three of them lived in an old brick house. Every day when Monica got home from school and the weather was good, she took Hamlet and Howard out to play. She put Hamlet's cage in the back yard where he could run around his exercise wheel in the sun. Then she and Howard ran through the woods. Monica galloped. Howard bit trees and chased yellow Ping-Pong balls.

"Mush, you husky!" Monica would yell as they ran through the woods. Monica trusted Howard more than anyone else in the world. He didn't tell secrets on her the way kids did, and he didn't laugh at her either. Not even when she turned nine and still pretended she was a horse.

Monica trusted Hamlet too, but there were limits to friendship with a hamster. All Hamlet did was run around his exercise wheel, sleep, eat, and go to the bathroom. He never gave joyful greetings and slobbery kisses when she came home, or put his furry head in her lap while he licked her arm. About the most he did was squeak when he was hungry, and sit in her hand when he ate his dinner.

"He doesn't do much, but he needs me to take care of him," she told Howard one day as they sat staring at the hamster. She scratched the dog's furry ears. "You need me too, don't you, Howard? To walk you and feed you and clean your ears and drown your fleas." She looked at him thoughtfully. "And I need you to keep me company and be my friend."

Sometimes, it seemed Howard was Monica's *only* friend.

"Why don't you play with Pamela today?" Mrs. Bottleby would ask.

"Because Pamela always wants to play her way instead of mine."

"I should think you could work out some

sort of compromise," Mrs. Bottleby would reply.

"I don't think so. It always seems like I do the giving, and Pamela does the taking."

There were, of course, kids on the block besides Pamela, but Monica didn't think they would be much fun either. Things got too complicated when kids were involved. Dealing with animals was simpler. "Hamlet and Howard need me," she told her mother. "Pamela doesn't."

So on sunny days she left Hamlet to play in the back yard while she ran through the woods, throwing Ping-Pong balls for Howard and pretending she was a horse. On rainy days the three of them stayed in her room and made a mess. And every Wednesday, Monica and Howard patrolled the block, looking for dead birds that had been squashed by cars. Monica held funerals for them in the woods. She brought Hamlet to the ceremonies in a shoe box full of cedar chips. Howard came on a leash so he wouldn't eat the birds. There were hundreds of things for a girl with a hamster and

a dog to do. Life was so full, Monica hardly ever had time to think about being lonely.

But for a common brown toad named Schultz, loneliness was all there was in life.

Schultz P. Toad lived in an empty terrarium in the back of Monica's classroom. Nobody paid much attention to him because all he did was sit in the corner and breathe. Sometimes he blinked, or stretched his feet, but that was it.

The kids in Monica's class played with him for a few days when he first arrived, and then they abandoned him in his terrarium next to a big pink conch shell and a jar full of dead snails. They thought he was boring. Only Monica and the teacher remembered to feed him.

Monica didn't just remember Schultz. She liked him. She liked the way his paunchy body ballooned when he breathed. She liked the stubby bumps on his back and she liked the way he scrunched his eyes down when he swallowed. Monica didn't think Schultz was boring at all.

"Why do you spend so much time with that silly old toad?" asked Pamela one day while Monica was taking care of him.

"He's not silly."

"Not silly? All he does is sit around and stare at things. Why don't you forget about him and come look at my new book? It's about horses, and it has tons of great pictures."

Monica hesitated. She loved horses. "I have to feed Schultz and clean his tank first," she said quietly.

Pamela frowned. "But then there won't be enough time left to look at my book. I'm taking it back home today."

"Oh," said Monica. "Maybe you could bring it back tomorrow?"

"Maybe," said Pamela. She made a face at the toad and rushed back to her desk.

Monica leaned over Schultz's terrarium. "If you'd *do* something once in a while, other kids would pay attention to you," she whispered as she gave him a bunch of live bugs. Schultz just looked at her. Why should he do anything in an empty glass box with no place to hide in, no place to hop to, and no other toads to stare at? Besides eating and sleeping, there was nothing to do except sit in the corner and breathe. From what Monica could tell, life was a bore as far as Schultz P. Toad was concerned. It dragged on month after dreary month until she couldn't stand watching any longer.

"Can Schultz come home and live with me?" she asked her science teacher.

"Yes," he said.

Monica's mother said yes too, so Schultz and his tank moved into Monica's room. He was another someone who needed to be taken care of, and Monica was sure she could make a home for him.

"Now all we have to do is fix up the terrarium," she announced to Hamlet and Howard. The hamster watched for a few seconds and then returned to cleaning his feet. Howard, on the other hand, was *absolutely fascinated*. Like a cat in the grass, he crouched on the floor, staring into Schultz's terrarium and drooling with delight onto Monica's arm.

"YUCK!" she screeched in her loudest, most

impatient voice. She shoved the big dog out of the room and locked the door.

Disgraced, he stood and stared mournfully at the closed door. Monica hadn't locked him out since he was a puppy who didn't know about not eating furniture and going to the bathroom on the rugs. She'd never lost her temper and shoved him out before. Howard wasn't even sure what he'd done wrong. He knew hamsters were off limits, but Monica had never said a word about toads. Now she was so preoccupied with her new pet that she completely forgot the dog waiting patiently outside.

"I'm going to make you a cave for hiding and a hill for climbing," Howard heard her say to Schultz, "and a pond for swimming and a moss field for hopping." She stayed in her room for what seemed like hours, and the time crawled by like a caterpillar. Howard stood in the hall and heaved one mournful sigh after another. Finally he lay down and closed his eyes. Paws twitching, he slept, until Monica exploded through the door and fell on him.

"Ooph!" she grunted. She sat up and grinned

at the sleepy creature beneath her. She'd already forgotten Howard's slobberiness, and her impatience was gone too. "Want to come downstairs with me?" she asked, with an affectionate tug at his hairy ears. "It's almost time for dinner."

Howard thumped his tail but didn't move.

There were things to be checked out while Monica was elsewhere. He waited until she walked into the bathroom and closed the door.

"Into the air, junior birdmen," she sang gaily as she washed her hands.

Howard stood up, stretched, and padded into Monica's room. The sun glared through the windows. He looked around, blinked, and froze. There, in the place of honor, sat the toad intruder, in a clear glass terrarium on Monica's night table. He was hopping in slow, deliberate circles, exploring the hills and valleys Monica had just built for him. Howard stalked purposefully toward him, pushed his nose down into the terrarium, and sniffed. It was a loud, hungry sniff, and Schultz P. Toad froze. He stared up at the big yellow teeth and hot pink tongue.

Schultz didn't have to be smart to know he was in big trouble. He flattened himself to the ground, but Howard snorted after him. Schultz's tiny body pounded with fear. Frantically, he dug himself backward into a hole. It didn't work. Howard nosed after him until his

tongue touched the toad's trembling body.
With an excited yip, Howard scooped the pet-
rified animal into his mouth and jumped from
the table.

If Schultz had been a hamster, that would have been the end of him. But Schultz was a toad, and there are poison glands in toad skin that make toad-eating a bad idea for most animals, including dogs. As soon as Howard grabbed him, the glands behind Schultz's eyes and in the bumps of his back oozed liquid poison. Howard's mouth felt horrible. He gasped, letting Schultz tumble onto the floor before he could even think about swallowing him. Then the dog bolted from the room, whining pathetically. He rushed down the hall — smack into Monica.

She had finally finished washing up. "Ninety-nine bottles of beer on the — HOWARD! What's the matter with you?" The dog looked up guiltily as he slunk downstairs to hide under the sofa. His owner looked from him to the bedroom. Everything clicked.

"Schultz!"

Monica raced to the terrarium and found Schultz lying motionless on the floor. She peered down at him. "Hey, Schultz P. Toad, are you all right?" The toad lay very still, but he was still breathing. She put him back in the terrarium and headed downstairs. Tears dribbled down her cheeks.

Best friend or not, Howard was in big trouble. He trembled beneath the sofa, refusing to move, even when Monica in her sternest voice ordered him to come out. She sat on the floor, leaned under the sofa, and shook her finger at him. "Howard," she said slowly, "leave the toad ALONE. Do you hear me? ALONE."

The dog looked up at her, his mouth still burning miserably. Nobody had to tell Howard to leave the toad intruder alone now. Toads were loathsome and foul-tasting and ugly. Howard didn't want anything more to do with them for as long as he lived. He closed his eyes against Monica and the world and sighed.

Two days went by. Every morning when Monica woke up, she peered into Schultz's tank to be sure he was still alive. And every afternoon when she got home from school, she ran upstairs and brought him mealworms. But Schultz just sat in the corner. He didn't move, and he didn't eat.

"It's Howard's fault," said Monica. So she locked Howard out of her room and stopped throwing Ping-Pong balls for him and stopped brushing his fur and cleaning his ears.

The big dog didn't understand. He followed her from room to room, only to have doors shut in his face. He lay patiently outside of them, waiting for Monica, the center of his world. But she was angry with him. She spent the days worrying about Schultz P. Toad.

It was fall, and there were still some bugs outside. Monica caught some and brought them home for Schultz. She lined them up in appetizing rows. He ignored them.

28

But after several long days, one looked so good he couldn't resist any longer. An especially plump mealworm crawled over Schultz's foot and the toad snapped to attention. He lurched forward and caught the worm with his long, sticky tongue. Then he scrunched his eyes and swallowed.

"He's all right! He's all right!" Monica cried joyously. She ran down the hallway, with Howard at her heels barking.

The toad intruder had survived.

From that day on, Schultz ate all the bugs Monica brought him, even when winter came and it was time for him to hibernate. Monica kept him interested in staying awake by keeping her room warm and feeding him live bugs. The bugs lived in a jar in the kitchen refrigerator—until four of them showed up on the leftover meat loaf.

"Leftovers are bad enough," said Mrs. Bottleby. "Bugs are out of the question." From then on, they stayed in dirt-filled boxes in the basement.

Winter crept by. Often it was too cold to

29

play outside, so Monica stayed in with her animals. Slowly, she forgave Howard for trying to eat Schultz. He had, after all, just done what dogs do naturally, and he seemed to have learned that toads were for watching, not eating. Perhaps she had been too hard on him.

"I'm sorry, Howard," she said one day as they sat on the floor together. She put her arms around the big dog's neck and hugged him. Howard buried her under a storm of slobbery kisses and barked joyfully in her ear.

Hamlet the hamster continued to dig through his cedar chips and run around and around his exercise wheel. But despite Monica's determined efforts to interest him in other activities, Schultz P. Toad still spent most of his time sitting in the corner, breathing. Life didn't seem to have changed much from his days in the back of Monica's science class, even though she'd fixed up the terrarium and paid lots of attention to him.

"I guess toads are like that," she told Howard one snowy February day as they sat in their usual spot. "He does even less than Hamlet does." She stared at the toad and the toad stared back with his beautiful gold-flecked eyes. Then he hunched forward and pulled his head toward the ground. The skin split down the center of his back and stomach, and across his chest.

"I can't believe it," gasped Monica. She stared as Schultz reached down, grabbed the nearest edge of broken skin in his mouth, and ate it.

Monica slammed her eyes shut and groaned. "I can't think of a more disgusting way to grow bigger," she muttered to Howard as she stalked quickly from the room. "I know that eating their skin is supposed to be good for them, but I'm going downstairs before I throw up." She spent the rest of the day cleaning bug boxes.

Schultz split his skin one more time before spring. When May came, he was big, bumpy, and beautiful. He was also grown up, and from someplace in his tiny brain a soft, persistent voice called him back to the woods and streams of his youth.

It was time for Schultz to find a mate.

"Schultz peeped last night," Monica told her mother one Saturday at breakfast.

"He's probably calling for a female," her mother replied.

"To make babies with?"

"Yes."

"But how?"

Mrs. Bottleby looked at her daughter thoughtfully. "Well, the female toad lays thousands of eggs in a long thin tube."

"*Thousands* of eggs?"

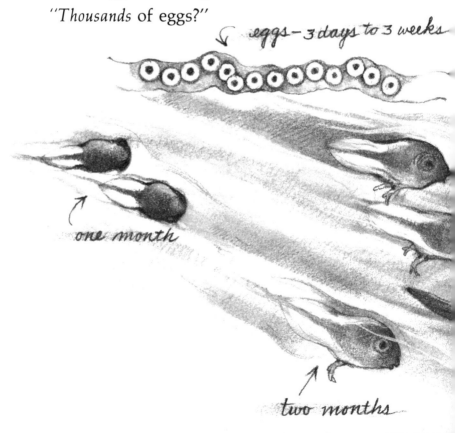

eggs – 3 days to 3 weeks

one month

two months

"It certainly is a lot, isn't it? But there have to be that many, because so many of them are eaten or lost before they hatch. Anyway, after the eggs are fertilized by a male, they float in the water until the sun warms them enough to hatch. Then they become tiny tadpoles, which live and breathe in the water like fish. After a while, they grow lungs and legs. Then the tadpoles are toads, and they leave the water to live on the land."

Monica's eyes widened. "Schultz couldn't possibly fit thousands of babies in his terrarium."

"I know," said her mother.

adult toad

three months

"And he doesn't have another toad to make tadpoles with," Monica continued.

"I know," repeated her mother softly.

Monica's stomach fluttered. She got up abruptly. "I think I want to go for a walk." She rinsed her dishes, called her dog, and headed for the woods. There, she marched blindly along, her mind cluttered with unpleasant thoughts.

"Schultz is mine," she said firmly, "and he needs me, and I love him, even if he is only a toad. He'd still be stuck in that stupid old classroom if it wasn't for me, and he'd probably have starved to death by now." She threw herself down on a log and stared glumly at the stream in front of her. The water danced under the sun and mumbled to the stones.

"Howard, I want to talk to you," she said. The dog came gladly, tail wagging. She scratched his muzzle.

"When you tried to eat Schultz, he tasted so bad you left him alone," she recalled quietly. "Mom says only a few kinds of animals, like skunks and snakes and owls, can eat toads. If a toad was very careful in these woods, he probably wouldn't have much to worry about." Howard handed her a grimy forepaw and panted.

"There are enough bugs here to eat, too," she added, flicking a beetle from her knee. She watched a box turtle sunning himself on a nearby rock. Her face tightened. "But he's *my* toad, Howard. He should stay in the terrarium where he belongs to me. If I put him outside, I'll never see him again." A tear strayed down her cheek. Howard whined.

"I don't think I like the woods today," she muttered. She got up and tramped toward home.

The morning drifted into afternoon, the afternoon into early evening. Monica sat in her room, staring at the sunset. The air felt soft and warm and the sky grew dark. She'd spent the entire day thinking about toads and hamsters and dogs and now she was tired. The windows were open, and a light breeze brushed against her face. On that breeze came the faint, high sound of toads singing in the distance.

"It's like a flute chorus," she whispered, "only it seems like part of the air itself." Even as she spoke, Schultz P. Toad peeped.

He was standing at rigid attention, listening to the sounds of the night.

Monica looked at him. She peeped back. But Schultz ignored her. He knew a real toad when he heard one. Monica watched him, and suddenly she felt very unimportant. She buried her face in the comforting softness of Howard's furry neck. They listened as the toads sang louder and louder and Schultz P. Toad answered. Finally, Monica could keep quiet no longer.

"I can't stand listening to them calling each other when Schultz is trapped in a little glass box. Maybe it's not right to keep him here with me. I've got to put him back." They were hard words for Monica to say, and they made her feel sort of helpless. She trudged downstairs.

Her mother hugged her gently when Monica told her what she planned to do. "Monica," she said, "it's not as bad as all that, you know. If you took Schultz back to the brook, he could find a mate and start life for hundreds of other toads. And if you went back to the brook again in a few weeks, you might catch a tadpole and bring it home. It could be one of Schultz's. We'd put it in a tank full of water and plants, with a big rock in the middle so when the tadpole got big enough to have legs and lungs it could crawl out of the water and live in Schultz's terrarium. It would take about three years for it to grow up and want to return to the brook to be with other toads for a while, and then you could start all over again. That is, if you wanted to."

"Do you think Schultz would be happier that way?" asked Monica in a trembling voice.

"Yes, I think he would."

Monica studied the floor for a while. Then she studied Howard's ear. "Does that mean I should let Hamlet go too?"

"Oh, I don't think so. Hamlet would have too many animals trying to eat him, and he seems quite content in his cage. Schultz is the one calling for a mate."

"Should I let him go tonight?"

"It's up to you, but the longer you wait, the harder it will become."

Minute upon lonely minute ticked by, and Monica made her decision. "I'll carry him in Hamlet's shoe box so he won't get hurt," she said at last. Then she fumbled through the darkness toward her closet.

"I'll get a flashlight and meet you downstairs," said Mrs. Bottleby.

Monica rubbed her sleeve over the tears sneaking down her cheeks. Then she picked up the shoe box and placed Schultz carefully inside. There were holes in the lid to let air through. She walked downstairs and met her mother at the back door.

"Is it O.K. for me to go alone?" asked Monica.

"If you take Howard with you."

So Monica, Howard, and Schultz P. Toad ventured into the warm, dark night. The woods pulsed with secret rustlings. Monica's flashlight beam flitted over the branches. "A person could get scared doing this kind of stuff," she

said aloud. Howard pushed against her and woofed. "Ssssh, Howard, we're here."

The stream glittered under the moonlight, and the toads became silent at their approach. Monica sat on her log and made Howard lie down. She put the shoe box on the ground, took off the lid, and laid the box on its side. Then she shut off the flashlight and waited patiently.

A minute went by . . . then five . . . then ten. Gradually the night noises returned, and the

toads called each other in the clear, dark water. There seemed to be hundreds of them.

Schultz sat upright, eyes bright, body straining. He hopped toward the stream. The air felt good, and the water cooled his bumpy skin. He sat in the shallows and sang to the night, his voice louder with each breath he took. Something moved at the edge of the stream. It was a female toad swimming toward Schultz. They found each other in the water, and Schultz groped clumsily for her. When he finally let go,

a single strand of fertilized eggs drifted from them and twisted around the weeds. There it would float until the sun brought life to the unborn tadpoles within.

Monica stood quietly, then walked home. She would come back in a few weeks, and there would be tadpoles. Some of them would be Schultz's.

"I think I'll be their aunt. A person can be a tadpole's aunt, can't she, Howard? I'll come back, and maybe I'll bring Pamela." She looked at Howard impishly. "It would be nice to spend some time with someone who talked back once in a while. All you ever do is agree with me!"

The dog wagged his tail and bumped against her. Together they walked through the woods. The toad chorus sang in their ears, and Monica smiled. Hamlet and Howard belonged with her, but she realized now that toads weren't meant to live in glass terrariums.

"Good-bye, Schultz," she whispered. Then she walked into the house with her dog and closed the door carefully behind her.